The snake that couldn't hiss

Written and illustrated
by
Shoo Rayner

Heinemann

C000088830

We all know that snakes hiss.
Well, this is a story about a snake
that could not hiss.
The snake was called Sneaker.

Wherever he went Sneaker made no noise at all. The other animals could never hear him coming.

But Sneaker could hear all the other
animals very well.
He could hear the other snakes hissing.

He could hear the grasshoppers singing.

And he could hear the frogs croaking.

One day Sneaker heard some snakes
hissing to one another. He wanted to
know what they were hissing about, so
he slid through the grass to see them.
He made no noise at all, so the snakes
didn't hear him coming.

'Hello!' said Sneaker.

'Oh Sneaker! You made us jump,' said
the snakes. 'You should hiss like us.
Then you wouldn't make us jump.'

'But I can't hiss,' said Sneaker sadly,
and he slid away through the grass.

Just then Sneaker heard some grasshoppers singing. He wanted to know what they were singing about, so he slid through the grass to see them. He made no noise at all, so the grasshoppers didn't hear him coming.

'Hello!' said Sneaker.
'Oh Sneaker! You made us jump,'
said the grasshoppers. 'You should
sing like us. Then you wouldn't
make us jump.'

Sneaker tried and tried to sing like
the grasshoppers, but it was no good.
He could make no noise at all.

'I can't sing,' said Sneaker sadly,
and he slid away through the grass.

Then Sneaker heard some frogs
croaking. He wanted to know what
they were croaking about, so he
slid through the grass to see them.
He made no noise at all, so the frogs
didn't hear him coming.

'Hello!' said Sneaker.

'Oh Sneaker! You made us jump,' said
the frogs. 'You should croak like us.
Then you wouldn't make us jump.'

Sneaker tried and tried to croak like
the frogs, but it was no good.
He could make no noise at all.

'I can't hiss. I can't sing. And I can't croak,' said Sneaker sadly. 'Oh why can't I make a noise?'

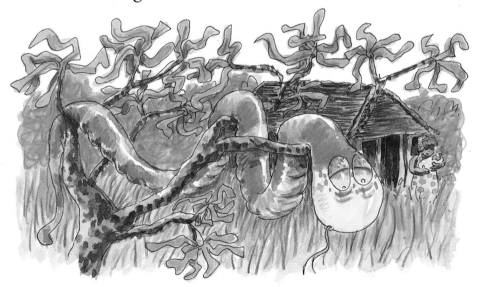

Sneaker was so sad that he went off to live on his own.

Then one day Sneaker was going
through the grass when he saw
something on the path. He pushed it
out of the way.
RATTLE.
'What was that?' said Sneaker.
'It made me jump!'

Sneaker looked down. It was a rattle.
Sneaker pushed the rattle with
his tail.
RATTLE. RATTLE.

Then Sneaker put his tail inside
the rattle.
RATTLE. RATTLE. RATTLE.
The noise grew louder.
'Wow!' said Sneaker. 'I must go and
show this to the other animals.'
And off he went.

All the other animals were talking to
one another when suddenly they heard,
RATTLE! RATTLE! RATTLE!
The noise grew louder and louder.
'Look!' they said. 'It's Sneaker.
He's a rattlesnake! Now we will
always hear him coming!'